Island Supply Delivery
(Every Other Friday)

DANGER!

Beachy's Migratory Route

SCHOOL CROSSING

WRECK OF THE H.M.S.

MYSTERY ROCK

The Lost Treasure of Armadastan

Beachy

The Bubble Chimneys

Pixie

ROBT T. STAAKE · MAPMAKER · CHATHAM·MASS

To George Costanza, marine biologist

Copyright © 2016 by Bob Staake
All rights reserved. Published in the United States by Random House Children's Books, a division of Penguin Random House LLC,
New York. Random House and the colophon are registered trademarks of Penguin Random House LLC.
randomhousekids.com
Educators and librarians, for a variety of teaching tools, visit us at
RHTeachersLibrarians.com
Library of Congress Cataloging-in-Publication Data
Names: Staake, Bob. author, illustrator.
Title: Beachy and me / by Bob Staake.
Description: First edition. | New York : Penguin Random House LLC, 2016 |
Summary: "It's summertime, but Pixie Picklespeare is lonely on the tiny island she
lives on with her family . . . until one day, when she makes friends with a
whale!"— Provided by publisher.
Identifiers: LCCN 2015018386| ISBN 978-0-385-37314-2 (hardback) |
ISBN 978-0-375-97198-3 (glb) | ISBN 978-0-375-98187-6 (ebk)
Subjects: | CYAC: Stories in rhyme. | Whales—Fiction. | Friendship—Fiction.
| Islands—Fiction. | BISAC: JUVENILE FICTION / Social Issues /
Friendship. | JUVENILE FICTION / Animals / Marine Life. | JUVENILE FICTION
/ Humorous Stories.
Classification: LCC PZ8.3.S778 Be 2016 | DDC [E]—dc23
The illustrations in this book were rendered in Adobe Photoshop.
MANUFACTURED IN CHINA
10 9 8 7 6 5 4 3 2 1   First Edition

BOB STAAKE

Beachy
and Me

Random House 🏠 New York

"This island's very tiny!"
cried Pixie Picklespeare.
"No wonder I'm so lonely—
I'm the only kid who's here!"

Cooped up inside the dinky house—
well, what could Pixie do?
She was bored with every board game,
and her jigsaw puzzles, too.

BORED

BORED

BORED

Burp!

Something big had come ashore.
It seemed to have a tail.
Pixie was now staring at . . .

a giant washed-up WHALE!

"Oh dear, this must look rather odd—
quite anything but peachy.
Apparently, I've washed ashore.
Hello—my name is Beachy!

"Just get me to the ocean, kid!
   That's where I need to be.
      And then I'll show you many games
         that we can play at sea!"

"I can help you!" Pixie cried,
but his skin bounced back
   like rubber.
She pushed the whale.
She heaved and shoved.

He just had too
much blubber!

"Oh, look, the tide is coming in—
it's time to catch our ride!
I'll be your true-blue friend, and then
your ocean playtime guide!"

Pixie made a big
KER-SPLASH
that soaked the rocks
with foam.

The sloshy waves washed Beachy free—
at last the whale was home!

Beachy taught her how to breach,

and ride tsunami waves.

Pixie learned to hold her breath
and swim through hidden caves!

They splished and splashed all summer long.
They made that ocean bubble!
They flipped and flopped and bobbed like corks—
a wet 'n' wild odd couple!

But then . . .

Beachy listened to his heart.
It told him, "Time to sail!"
He had to migrate once a year
to be with other whales.

"Don't worry, Pixie," Beachy said.
"We'll soon be back at play.
I'll always be your true-blue friend,
and I'll return one day."

Pixie moped around the house.
She missed her giant friend. . . .
The smiles they'd shared, the laughs, the fun—
oh, why'd it have to end?

MOPE
MOPE
MOPE

Splash!

Pixie grabbed her lighthouse beam.
She shined it through the black.
She cast it on a wave and saw . . .

that
Beachy
had
come
back!

"I kept my promise, Pixie.
I'm back to play with you!
And now we'll meet here every year—

like old friends often do!"

Scale
1 Inch = 20 Feet

PIXIE'S ISLAND

AND SURROUNDING OCEAN ENVIRONS

Picklespeare
Lighthouse
(Built 1893)

Great
Candy Cane
Coral
Reef

ATLANTIS CLIPPER CURRENT

Southern
Sea Caves

Sunrise
Beach

Sunset
Beach

THE TIDAL SHALLOWS

The Great
Kelp Forest
of Oceana